MW00953268

Dedication

For all of the little ones who aspire to be healthy, creative,

inclusive, and impactful: dream big and take a chance!

To our families, friends, and supporters: you all made this possible.

Thank you, and be healthy.

www.mascotbooks.com

Bizy Buddies Explore Digestion

For more information, please contact:
Mascot Books
620 Herndon Parkway, Suite 320
Herndon, VA 20170
info@mascotbooks.com

Library of Congress Control Number: 2020913704

CPSIA Code: PRTWP1220A

ISBN-13: 978-1-64543-738-3

Printed in South Korea

Bizy Buddies

Explore Digestion

Written by Kevin Kohlstedt and Rudy Valenta

Do you know where food goes in your belly?
It is quite a trip and might end smelly!
The Bizy Buddies will be our guide
As we explore what's going on inside.

Now, we've eaten carrots, avocados, and peas.
The digestion journey starts down toward our knees.
The Bizy Buddies use the nutritious food we ate
To make energy that helps us grow strong and great.

Chew, chew, swallow;
Down it will go!
Remember step one—chew like a goat!
Swallow, and then down into the throat,
Food moves past our lungs, past the heart and chest.
Bizy Buddies make sure it passes the test!

Next stop is the stomach—it's like a big pool
Where Bizy Buddies splash and try to stay cool.
Good gut bacteria breaks down our food
To smaller bits that go down the next tube.

Splish, splash, splish, splash!
The Bizy Buddies mix, and Bizy Buddies mash.

These hard workers send thanks as little burps,
When we chew our food and our belly works.

Eager Bizy Buddies now pick and choose with care—
Vitamins and nutrients grabbed here and stored there.
Citrus fruits keep you healthy with Vitamin C;
Nuts and fish boost your brain with Omega-3s.

Grunt, grunt, grunt—Bizy Buddies start to bumble.
Calcium for strong bones to protect you in a tumble.

Proteins build muscles, vitamins for healthy hair and skin;
Drinking lots of water makes all the gears spin.
And while sugar tastes nice when we enjoy a treat,
Only have one piece, or it will knock you off your feet.

When we eat healthy food, these Bizy Buddies can tell.
They give us energy to play and ring the fun bell!

Next in the large intestine, strong Bizy Buddies push,
Compacting things, cheering, and yelling, "Mush mash mush!"
They combine all the bits our body doesn't need.
Good thing we ate all those fruits, veggies, and greens.

Fiber promotes movements that are soft and smooth
For the next big step, where it all goes down the luge.

Now, into your colon where everything sits and waits.
It's almost time for the Bizy Buddies to drop the crates.

When you feel it's the right time in your day,
Gently push to send your poop on its way!

High fives, cheers, hip hip, hooray!
Look at how much we have learned today.
You and the Bizy Buddies all celebrate.
We explored digestion, and you did great!

Kevin Kohlstedt believes in a sustainable world and develops solar energy projects that help fuel the clean energy future for his daughter, five nephews, and niece. He has worked as a janitor, lifeguard, developer, landscaper, and infrastructure engineer. He and his family live in Santa Monica, California with a gentle sea breeze and constant drive to explore the endless beauty of the outdoors.

Rudy Valenta believes that children are our future and that their education is the key to creating change. He has been a grocery store stockist, bartender, restaurant cook, and children's toy designer. He loves to run races, make instant ramen, and is currently learning how to become a better swimmer. He and his partner live in Brooklyn, New York with a wall full of books and a collection of plants to keep their urban life green.

Thank you to all of our generous supporters!

Isabelle Adams Ryan Alberts Brad Albrecht Laura Ashley Allan Clea Alsip Amy Ancona Trevor Anderson Brittany Ann Kristen Lynn Arnold Patricia Bagwell Jamie Balayti Jen Baldassarre Megan Baldassarre Barb and Paul Baldassarre Kate Balderston Joey and Caitlin Bardos John and Amy Bastian Jack and Ann Becker Kristen Becktel Carolann Belk Mihir Bhangley Dylan Binkley Danny Binstock Richard Bird Ignacio Blanco Alex Blouin Aaron, Kristin, Grayson, and Francesca Bowling Lizz Brann Andrew Braun Kevin and Bruce Brinkman Collin Bruck Donna Bulliard Maggie Buysse Colleen Caplice Sean Carr Patrick Caughey Linda Chan Elaine Chen Sue Yee Chen Alex Chiang Kyle Chisholm Kay and Craig Chisholm Ryan Chong Sol Christensen Megan Christenson Naomi Clayman Laura Connor Abbie, Mark, Sam and Maxine Cooke Andrew Corcoran Edwin Corlett Kaitlin and Eric Curry Michael De Runtz Katie De Runtz Tom Dillon Ted Dimiropoulos Anil and Julia Divakaran Sanjay Divarkaran Kristen Dold Ashley, Johnny and Rosie Ehmann Kevin Elberts Arel English Don Eschenauer Jane and John Evans Geoff Fallon Lois Fisher Julie Fitzpatrick Jackie Flaherty Michelle Flores Meghan Freebeck Rachel Freund Bryanna and Troy Friedlander Mike Fung Ray, Meghan, Nora and Flynn Gage Mike and Katie Genaze Meagan Geurts Phillip Goodman Rebecca Goodrich Joel and Bethany Grachan Joe Green Steve Guinee Samantha Gurrola Kim and Peter Guse Patrick Healy Brian Herbolich Paul Hildebrand Albert Hill Ben Hilton Adam and Becca Hines Julia Hitzbleck Sheila Ho Ryan Hoch Travis, Tyler and Quinn Hodgson Brianca Holland Ben Hoogheem Xiaoyue Hou Anastasia Hou Jon Hric Leigha Huggins Sheila Jackson Susan Jania Danielle Javier Maisie Jean Krakowski Josh Jennrich Geoff Johnson Chris and Lindsay Kammo Katie Kamykowski Todd Kantarek Greg Karolich Keri Keasal Robert Keller Andrew Kim Garrett Klein Jackie Klein Dewey Klurfield Shayne Zotti Koch Chris Koenig Jim and Pat Kohlstedt Matt, Sarah, Ben and Zoe Kohlstedt Karly and Avery Kohlstedt John Kosir Rachel Kunz Grant and Sue Kuphall Seongjin Kwon Michael Lahris Ximena Beltran Larkin Ryan Larkin Dan Lee Patrick Leibach Dani Levy Walsh Christen Love Peter Lucas Mila "Meimei" Luna Matt Lynch Jill Lyons Allie Mabbot Sarah Macchia Timothy Maier Ben Manuel Tracie Marie Sarah Marion Meg Marsh James Marsh Clare Marsh Alison Marvel Connor and Danielle McCarthy Nansi McCay Peter McElligott Julia and Mitch McGilliard Thomas, Erin and Hunter McHardy Kristen McMillin Liska Annie McQuillan David Mesri Lindsey, Devin, Will and Luke Meyer Natalie Mikat-Stevens Justin Miller Whitney Moeller Archith Mohan Max Molloy James Moore Ben, Bonny and Everly Mundt Bryan Musolf Reid Myers Natalie and Danny Napleton Tedd, Pauline and Milo Notari Kevin O'Brien Danny and Marina O'Connor Jen Opie Hewsan Pang Karen Park Hannah and Jax Park Tripp Parran Brigette Pease Tony and Erin Perrino Sarah Phillips Helen Poladyan Alex Polzin Katie, Paco, Kai and Teo Portillo Kohlstedt Cynthia and Luke Powers Print Ninja Adam Record Preethi Reddy Lindsay Reiche Nathan Reid Linda Reid Chris and Christina Komperda Ricciardi Don and Jenn Richman Corinne Richman and Alex Liker Ryan Riordan Melanie Suelie Rios Muffy Robinson King Gina and Joe Rossi Jillian Ruggiero-Gaza Tyler Sanchez Marisa Scavo Joe Scavuzzo Matt Schafer Jon Semingson Patrick Shannon Jack and Alicia Shannon Sam Ian Slaughter Joe Slotnick Carolyn and Matt Snider Bryant Soong Andrew Staniec Cameron Stewart Julie Stromsburg Rosemary Stuebi Kristina Sullivan Kenneth Sullivan Esther Sung Stanley Tack Trish Taylo The Creative Fund Stephy Thomas Jay Tighe Page Tighe Kelly Togashi Thomas Tredennick Sarah Trilla Isabel Tsai Dan Turtle Alex Tutt Rudy and Noriko Valenta Joellen Valentine Mateo Valentino Jenna Verdicchio Kosin Virapornsawan Erica Virtue Nick and Lauren Vissat Christie Volden Anne Waling Joe, Sara and Juniper Walsh Dan and Allie Walters Michelle Wei Nick Wilson Erin Winner Koki Wu Leona Yi-Fan Su Sung Yoo Rev Dave and Sue Zelgart Ryan and Cal Zelgart Claire Zeng Ashley Zorrilla Allison Zuzelo

 @bizybuddies

 @bizybuddies

 @bizybuddies